Linda Jennings was born in Sussex and now lives in North London with her six cats. One of her cats is Tabby Max, seen in the photograph on the back cover. Besides cats, Linda likes reading, classical music, walking and collecting antiques. She has written many children's books and works as a children's book editor.

Martin Ursell was born in Fulham, London and now lives with his wife in Surrey. He has two cats and a pet frog called Fatima. As well as illustrating many children's books, Martin teaches at Chelsea School of Art and regularly works for the BBC on *Jackanory*. In his spare time, he enjoys gardening.

British Library Cataloguing in Publication Data
Jennings, Linda M. (Linda Marion), *1937 –*
    Tabby Max
    I. Title   II. Ursell, Martin, *1958 –*
    823'.914[J]
    ISBN 0-7214-9594-X

First edition

Published by Ladybird Books Ltd Loughborough Leicestershire UK
Ladybird Books Inc Auburn Maine 04210 USA
© Text LINDA JENNINGS MCMLXXXIX
© LADYBIRD BOOKS LTD MCMLXXXIX
Printed in England

Tabby Max

by LINDA JENNINGS
illustrated by MARTIN URSELL

Ladybird Books

Tabby Max was a very ordinary cat. He had four white paws and a white smudge on his nose. He had little tabby bracelets round his legs. He belonged to a lady called Betty who loved him very much. He had his own cat basket and a pink cat-nip mouse.

Sometimes Tabby Max felt his life was a bit dull. Sometimes he wished he was like his sister, Sophie, who lived with a witch. It would be so much more exciting than playing with a cat-nip mouse.

One evening Tabby Max saw something very exciting on television. It was an enormous animal, yellow with black stripes, and a set of ferocious-looking teeth.

'That's a tiger,' said Betty. 'He's a kind of relation, you know.'

Related to a tiger. Me? Tabby Max sat up and practised a snarl. He lashed his tail from side to side.

'You'll never be a tiger in a thousand years,' laughed Betty.

Tabby Max did not like being laughed at. He laid
back his ears and banged out of the cat-flap. He'd
show her! He would become a proper tiger. He
would go to visit his sister, Sophie. She would know
what to do, for she had learned a bit of magic from
the witch. Off he trotted, deep into the woods, until
he reached the old cottage where Sophie lived.

'I don't know if I can make you into a whole tiger,' said Sophie.

'Half a tiger's no good,' said Tabby Max.

'I mean, I can make you *look* like a tiger, but you'll still feel like a cat.'

'It's the appearance that counts,' said Tabby Max.

'Well, I *suppose* I'm a tiger,' thought Tabby Max, as
he crashed back through the woods. 'I suppose those
huge stripy paws belong to me.' Tabby Max practised
a roar. A neighbour's dog, out in his garden for a late
night sniff, howled horribly and fled indoors. 'Wow!'
thought Tabby Max. 'I must be no end of a terrifying
fellow!'

He hurried across the lawn towards his cat-flap. He pushed at it with his nose, and there, in the moonlit kitchen, he saw his supper on what seemed to be a very small plate. He tried to get his head through the flap. He pushed and he squeezed, but it was no good. Tabby Max couldn't understand it at all.

The only other way in was through the landing
window. Tabby Max gave an enormous leap and
landed on the sill. Within seconds he was down the
stairs and into the kitchen. He stared hard at the
mouse-sized plate of food. With one gulp it was
gone. Tabby Max decided to tell Betty that he
needed some more.

Betty was fast asleep. Tabby Max put his front paws on her bed. It was strange, he thought, that his back legs remained on the ground.

'Miaow,' he said, plaintively. At least, that was what he meant to say.

But instead, he gave his enormous tiger-roar!

'AHH!' screamed Betty. 'HELP! A TIGER! SHOOT HIM, SOMEONE!'

A book hit Tabby Max on the side of his head.

Tabby Max fled down the stairs. What had he done?
Didn't Betty love him any more? He ran straight into
the dining room and squeezed himself under the
dresser. It was his favourite hiding place, but he had
great difficulty now in getting all of himself out of
sight. From under the dresser Tabby Max could hear
Betty telephoning someone.

'Is that the police?... Yes, a tiger. In my bedroom. No of *course* it's not a cat. I've a dear little tabby and I know what cats look like. You'll phone the zoo?... Very well. I'll keep the beast at bay. AAH! I can see his tail sticking out from under the dresser. Come at once, before he eats me!' Tabby Max looked at his huge stripy paws.

He suddenly realised why Betty was so frightened. Of course, he was now a tiger, though he didn't feel like one. Tabby Max crawled out from under the dresser, and purred loudly. 'I'm a *friendly* tiger,' he tried to tell her, but Betty ran to the door and opened it wide.

'Go *out*, you horrible beast,' she shouted. 'SHOO!'

Tabby Max shot out of the door and across the lawn.

He hid himself behind the summer house and thought hard. If Betty was going to call him a horrible beast and shout at him then he didn't want to be a tiger any more.

He peered round the edge of the summer house and could see some men with torches coming across the lawn. Betty was with them.

'There he is, Inspector. Behind the summer house,' said Betty. 'I can see his eyes gleaming.'

'Don't worry, Madam, the zoo keeper has a stun-gun. We'll soon lay him out and get him to the zoo in no time. It won't hurt him, just send him to sleep.'

Lay him out? Send him to sleep? Tabby Max was terrified. If he made a dash for it perhaps he could get safely to the woods. Then Sophie could change him back into an ordinary tabby. Tabby Max crept quietly away from the summer house, when PING! he felt a sharp prick in his side, his legs collapsed under him, and he knew no more until...

Tabby Max woke to find himself looking out at the
world through heavy bars. He was in a yard, with a
stunted tree, and a large shed behind him. There was
no way in which he could escape.

Tabby Max roared miserably. Where was his nice
garden? Where was Betty? Where was his special
salmon-flavoured cat food? He roared and he roared.

Now it so happened that the witch and Sophie were flying by overhead on their broomstick.

'That's a very unhappy tiger down there,' said the witch. 'I think we had better fly down and see what's wrong.'

'You stupid cats,' cried the witch when she heard what had happened. 'I've a good mind to change you both into toads.'

But as she was an old softie, despite her huge nose with a wart on it, she changed Tabby Max back into a cat instead.

'Now,' said the witch briskly. 'On the broomstick with you!'

Closing his eyes and feeling terribly sick, Tabby Max flew over the treetops until, with one eye open, he spotted his own garden far below him.

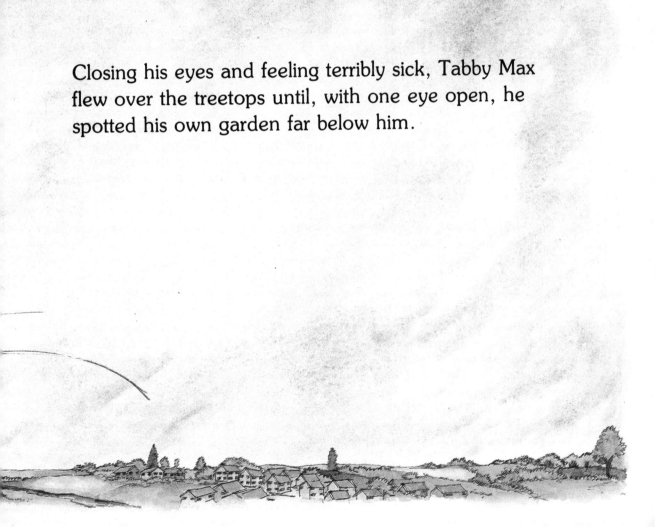

Five minutes later he had jumped off the broomstick
and was speeding across the lawn and through his
cat-flap. He ran straight through to the sitting room,
and jumped onto Betty's lap.

'Maxi!' cried Betty. 'So you weren't eaten by that horrible tiger!'

She tickled him under the chin in just the way he liked. Tabby Max purred and purred. He was home again with Betty, who loved him for the tabby cat he was.